PALACE
PUPPIES

PREVIOUSLY IN THE

PALACE PUPPIES

SERIES

Sunny and the Royal Party

Sunny to the Rescue

Sunny and the Snowy Surprise

PALACE PUPPIES

Sunny and the Secret Passage

MCDOUGAL

By Laura Dower

Illustrated by John Steven Gurney

DISNEP • HYPERION BOOKS
NEW YORK

Text copyright © 2013 by Laura Dower
Illustrations copyright © 2013 by John Steven Gurney

Printed in the United States of America
First Edition
10 9 8 7 6 5 4 3 2 1
V475-2873-0-13274

Library of Congress Cataloging-in-Publication Data
Dower, Laura.
Sunny and the secret passage / by Laura Dower; illustrations by John Steven Gurney. — First edition.
    pages cm.—(Palace puppies; 4)
Summary: Princess Annie's puppy Sunny, who likes to follow the rules, and Prince James's puppy Rex, who loves mischief, look for hidden treasure in McDougal Palace.
ISBN-13: 978-1-4231-6488-3
ISBN-10: 1-4231-6488-1
[1. Buried treasure—Fiction. 2. Castles—Fiction. 3. Dogs—Fiction.
4. Animals—Infancy—Fiction. 5. Behavior—Fiction. 6. Princes—Fiction.
7. Princesses—Fiction.] I. Gurney, John Steven, 1962– illustrator.
II. Title.
PZ7.D75458Suo 2013
[Fic]—dc23   2013012651

Visit www.disneyhyperionbooks.com

For the pup in Vero
who gets the royal treatment,
Miss Lily

—L.D.

To Gregg,
who loves Puppies!
Puppies! Puppies!

—J.S.G.

Chapter 1

What a storm!

An angry wind howled around the trees. I heard the rain click-clack against the window. A bolt of lightning brightened the gray sky over McDougal Palace.

Quickly, I dove under a couch. The only thing poking out was the tip of my yellow tail. But Rex must have seen a golden tuft. He grabbed the end of it and tugged hard.

"*ROWF!*" I wailed loudly.

"*Rowf,* yourself!" Rex barked back at me. "Quit hiding and come out! Blix and I are doing a rain dance to make it rain even harder! It's not

1

the same unless you do it with us."

I wiggled back out. "Fine," I barked, and got up on my hind legs. I made myself as tall as I could and shook my front paws. I loved to dance! It was even better with music.

Rex laughed at me. "Looking good!" he barked. "Now the rain will never, ever stop!"

Blix twisted and shook his ears from side to side. *"Wheeeee!"*

I smiled. "You're a pretty good dancer, too, Blix," I said. And I meant it.

Blix was the new pup in McDougal Palace. He was a furry white-brown-black husky who used to live up on Glimmer Mountain at the Winter Palace. He had grown up in a barn there with the other working huskies in his family. But Blix had a big secret: he had never liked being a dog who spent most of his time working outside.

On a snowy weekend trip to the Winter Palace, Rex and I met Blix. He decided he wanted to become an *inside* dog like us, instead of a working dog like his brother, Axel, and his sister, Chase. After a while, Princess Annie and Prince James figured out his secret. They decided to adopt Blix, and he moved to McDougal Palace to be with us.

Blix got used to palace life very quickly. Even though we were all different, it felt like we were meant to be siblings. Rex was a wild beagle who loved mischief. I was a goldendoodle who liked to follow the rules. And Blix was somewhere in between.

The more palace puppies in McDougal Palace the better!

Of course, Blix wasn't the only new thing at McDougal Palace. Our home was growing—and changing—more than ever before. A few months ago, the king and queen had a baby girl. They named her Rose. Princess Annie and Prince James loved their new sister.

"Come on, Sunny!" Rex barked loudly. "Dance like you have fleas!"

"Rex!" I giggled, falling back down onto all fours.

"Wag it! Wag it!" Blix cheered me on. He showed me a cool move that he'd learned while working the dog sled at the Winter Palace. He called it the ice slide.

"Woo-hoo!" I loved learning Blix's funky dance move. He really was one *cool* pup.

We were having a barking good time, but Annie didn't like all the commotion we were making inside the library. She held a finger to her mouth and looked right at *me*.

"Puppies must be quiet in the castle, Sunny. Shhhhhh!"

Rex snickered. "Yeah, quiet, Sunny!" he said, mocking me. He and Blix pounced onto a pile of pillows nearby. I lay down in front of the warm fire and rested my snout on my paws.

Prince James piled on another log and poked at it with one of the fireplace shovels. Embers shifted. Hot white sparks flashed within the stone walls of the fireplace.

"Watch out!" Prince James warned.

I scooted backward. Rex and Blix did, too.

A few sparks twisted out in front of the fireplace screen.

Princess Annie jumped up and came over to us. "James, you almost got sparks on the puppies! Be careful!"

I nuzzled her side. Thank you, Annie, I thought. *My princess always comes to my rescue.*

James just rolled his eyes.

"I *am* careful, Annie. I have my Outdoor Badge from the Scout Patrol. I know what I'm doing! And besides, Rex is fine. All the puppies are fine."

Annie crossed her arms. "You have to be even *more* careful now, with the new baby," she told James.

The arrival of puppy Blix had changed some things at the palace. But the arrival of baby Princess Rose had changed everything. All anyone ever wanted to talk about was Princess Rose. All anyone ever seemed to do was get things for Rose and worry about Rose.

But not everything about Princess Rose was rosy.

Rose didn't like to sleep much. She cried a lot, and not ordinary crying, either. Princess Rose made these loud shrieks. And she spat up all the time. Just yesterday, I got too close to Nanny Sarah while she was dressing the baby. Princess Rose nearly spat up on my head!

When James finished poking around at the hearth, Annie told us to settle back by the fire.

"I have a treat for you three," she said.

"Maybe we can roast marshmallows," Blix barked softly. "I remember doing that at the Winter Palace."

"The flames look so cool," Rex whispered to me with an orange glint in his eyes.

"Rex," I warned. I knew what that glint meant. "Flames are hot, not cool. Don't get any ideas!"

It's not really my *job* to watch the other pups. Watching pups was officially a job for the nannies. But goldendoodles are born helpers, even if no one asks us to help out. I usually tried to keep an eye on things when I could.

Ka-boom!

A thunderbolt crackled in the air outside the castle. It made so loud a noise that a log shifted in the fireplace! More orange-and-yellow sparks flew up. The rain beat hard against the large picture window.

Pitter-pat, pat, pat.

"I guess our rain dance worked," Rex joked to Blix.

All at once, I got that feeling I got whenever I jumped into a basket of freshly dried laundry. It was as if there were electricity in the air. All the little hairs on my tail stood up.

"Waaaaaaaaaaaaaaaaaaaa!"

From down the hall came a wail like a siren.

"Waaaaaaaaaaaaaaaaaaaa!"

Oh, no! Was that Princess Rose? She'd probably heard the same loud roar of thunder that had scared us—and woken right up. Thankfully, the nannies calmed her down again. We didn't hear a peep after that.

"Are you puppies ready to read?" Annie asked.

She curled up into the large red upholstered chair and lifted an embossed leather book from the end table. The book was covered with gold, purple, and green jewels that glimmered in the firelight.

A History of McDougal Palace

Wow! Annie could barely hold the book up to show us the pages. It was that big!

I'd never seen such a fancy book. Gold-flecked artwork on the front showed a castle with large birds flying overhead. A cluster of tall evergreen trees was painted next to its stone walls like some kind of mysterious and shadowy forest. Up high in one of the castle's towers, a yellow light shone brightly.

I knew this palace. This was McDougal Palace, our home.

"That book's been sitting on Dad's desk forever," James said, collapsing onto a sofa.

"I know. I asked him if I could borrow it. I thought we could read a story out loud to the pups," Annie said. "It's the perfect thing to do on a rainy day."

"*Ruff! Ruff!*" I barked excitedly. I understood everything Annie was saying. Reading *was* the perfect thing to do, on any day.

Rex didn't look so excited. "Sunny, I don't want to read. I want to run!"

"Rex," I whispered, "Annie's stories always give us the best doggy dreams. Let's listen for a little while at least."

"Sunny's right, Rex," Blix agreed. "I really want to hear about the palace. After all, I only just got here. I bet there are a lot of good stories about this place."

"Okay," Rex mumbled. He knew he was outnumbered. "We'll listen."

"*A long, long time ago,*" Annie said in a low voice, "*when dragons lived in the seas and enormous monsters roamed the dark forests—*"

"*ROWF!*" Rex barked happily. Of course he liked anything about monsters.

Now Annie had his full attention. Rex, Blix, and I inched closer to Annie's chair and listened carefully.

"*—there was a forbidden, faraway place called Glimmer Rock,*" Annie went on.

"Hey! That's where we live!" James said.

Annie shot him a look. "Yes, it's where we live," she said. She settled back with the book and kept reading. "*And in this place, a mysterious old man named Duff McDougal built a stone castle high on the cliffs of Glimmer Rock. He declared himself king of all the land and sea.*"

"Hold on!" James cried.

Annie grimaced. "What now?"

"The very first king of this palace was related to us?" Prince James asked.

"Yes! King Duff McDougal was our great-great-great-*great*-grandfather," Princess Annie replied.

"Uh . . . that's . . . er . . . *great!*" James cracked.

I chuckled to myself, but Annie made a face at him.

"Can I finish now?" she said. James nodded. "So! *King Duff established the kingdom of Glimmer Rock with his wife, Queen Veronica, and his children, Spence, Summer, Autumn, and Rose.*"

"Rose!" Rex and Blix cried out at the same time. Now they knew the baby princess had been named after one of her ancestors.

"*Inside the castle, King Duff built the perfect rooms for his children and his animals to play in.*"

"Animals, too?" Rex panted. We needed to know more about that part!

"*King McDougal loved his dogs,*" Annie went on. "*Just like I love you, Sunny, Rex, and Blix! So throughout McDougal Palace, he made special, hidden places for them. The king built passageways and scattered clues for his children and their pets all over the castle. They were encouraged to roam around the palace and find all sorts of—*"

"*ROWF!*" I barked. What I meant, of course, was *trouble.*

"Sunny! *Shhhh!*" Annie scolded me. "No barking! As I was saying . . . *the children were encouraged to find all sorts of secrets in the castle,*" Annie continued. "*The king even made a map for them to follow. Some say he left clues inside the castle walls. But the legend also says that once a puppy traveled behind the brick and stone, there was a great chance that pup might never be seen again.*"

I shuddered. Outside, the rain was coming down even harder than before. The doggy dancing had worked its magic. The storm surrounded

the castle with rumbling thunder and streaks of lightning across the sky.

Luckily, Princess Rose didn't wake up again from all the loud booms.

Princess Annie read to us for a very long time after that, until our heads got a little tired and our eyes got droopy. She told us a long, dreamy story about McDougal Gardens. She read a poem written by a queen named Joan. But after a while, Annie began to read more slowly than before. The beat of the raindrops on the windows grew steady as a drum. Annie let out an enormous yawn.

Before too long Annie was out cold, fast asleep.

James had fallen asleep, too. Boy, did he snore! The prince sounded like the palace lawn mower.

Of course, we all knew the princess and prince needed their sleep. Things at McDougal Palace had been so busy since Princess Rose arrived. Babies were exhausting!

Once Annie's body relaxed, she let go of the storybook about McDougal Palace. It dropped like a rock onto the carpeted floor. *THUNK!*

"I've never heard that story about the secret passage," Rex said.

"What if it was true?" Blix asked.

"Rex and I have lived in this palace for ages," I said to Blix. "I knew there were secret places to go, like through that door in Annie's closet. But I didn't really think the palace mysteries were this interesting."

"What if we look more closely for ways to walk inside the castle walls?" Rex said, twitching an ear.

I bit on the edge of a red woolen blanket that was on the sofa. Blix grabbed a green blanket and shook it in his mouth, too.

"Let's put these blankets on Annie and James and put the book back onto the table," I said, dragging the blanket with my teeth. "When Annie wakes up, we can read some more of the story together. . . ."

"I'll get the book," Rex volunteered. He opened his mouth wide so he could grab the book and carry it back to the table.

"Hey! It's too big for you to do that!" I scolded him. "And the book is heavy. It'll fall apart if you bite it or push it or—"

Rrrrrrrrrrrrrrip.

"Uh-oh!" Rex said. He took a few steps back from the book once he heard the rip. "I didn't mean to drop it. I'm sorry. . . ."

It was too late for apologies! A large tear ran along the inside cover of the enormous book.

"*Rowf!* Is it ruined?" Blix cried.

Quickly, we used our wet noses to shove the loose pages back inside the front of the book. But it was so hard to do! And just when we thought it was sort of fixed, another scrap of paper slipped to the floor.

This small, yellowed piece of folded paper was quite unlike the other pages.

"What's *this*?" I asked.

Gently, I unfolded the strange piece of paper with the tip of my nose, holding down a corner with my paw.

"Whoa!" Rex cried, nudging me out of the way. He pressed his paws onto the paper and smoothed out the crinkles.

"It's a map!" Blix said.

"No, it's *the* map!" I corrected him. "This is the map Annie told us about, from the book."

Chapter 2

The very top of the map read MCDOUGAL PALACE, EST. 1780.

Every room and space shown on the map had been clearly marked. There were some familiar places from the McDougal Palace we knew, like the gallery and the kitchen and the many bedrooms. But there were just as many *unfamiliar* places here, too.

"What's a B-U-T-T-E-R-Y?" Rex asked. "Some special room in the castle for making butter? Mmmmmm. Butter."

I found a map key on the side. It listed details about each of the rooms.

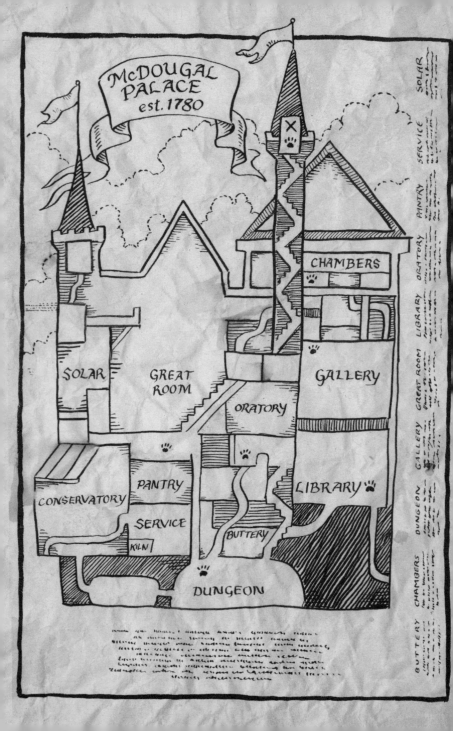

"*A buttery is a room for bottles,*" I read aloud. Another strange but large room was marked SERVICE, with an object in it labeled KILN, which I discovered was an old-fashioned word for *oven*.

There were oblong-shaped rooms and too-long hallways and secret passages.

It really came in handy being such a good reader!

A room with a wall of windows was labeled CONSERVATORY. At the lowest level of the castle was a space marked DUNGEON.

"Oooh, we should probably stay away from that place," I said. I'd heard creepy stories about dungeons.

"We can't stay away from any of these rooms!" Rex cried. "I want to explore! Let's use the map and see what we find! This could be the best real-life adventure ever!"

"Rex is right," Blix said. "It's great to explore new places outside. But exploring *inside* this castle will be way, *way* more fun than pulling a sled through the snow!"

Rex and I smiled. This was going to be fun.

At the tip-top of the McDougal Palace map was a small room with a big *X* in its center. Unlike the other rooms, this one did not have a label.

There was a golden paw print under the *X*.

"Ooooh!" I gasped.

Blix put his paw on the *X*.

"Hmmmmm," Rex said, sniffing the map as if that might produce some valuable information.

I'd seen an *X* on a map only once before, when Prince James had a pirate-themed birthday party. The king and queen had made up special maps for all the children. *X* on each map marked the spot where the party loot could be found. James's birthday treasure was located in the palace greenhouse. There were little colored pails filled with candy for all the guests. I remembered because that day Annie let me taste licorice for the first time.

Yuuuuuuummmy!

"Wait!" I exclaimed. "What if the *X* means there's treasure hidden in this castle?"

"Treasure?" Rex said.

"I knew this would be the best adventure ever," Blix added. "I wonder what the treasure could be."

I wondered, too. Was it a box of gold coins or a roomful of jewels? Or maybe there was a hidden stash of dog toys from the days of King Duff?

Our imaginations had no limits when it came to dreaming about all the things we could find on a tour of the palace.

"Maybe we will find a secret room filled with delicious dog bones," Blix dreamed aloud.

"Forget bones," Rex said. "I want a room filled with bacon!"

"Rex!" I yelped. "Let's not get carried away!"

But of course, my mouth started to water the moment he said *bacon*.

"What if there's a mystery room with a machine to rub our tummies?" Blix said.

"That makes me ticklish just thinking about it," I said, rolling around on my back on the carpet. We all giggled together.

"Hey, I just had a really scary thought," Rex said. "What if there's a family of *cats* inside the palace walls?"

"Bite your tail!" I blurted out.

At the Winter Palace, I'd had quite enough cat time with Fitzsimmons, the queen's cat. He'd tried to trick us at every turn and managed to get all us pups forced out of the house and into the drafty barn! Luckily, we'd made it home safe—no thanks to Fitz.

"Okay, let's get serious. If we are going to

explore, we'd better make a real plan," I said, pressing gently on the map with my paws.

The three of us took a closer look at all the details on this amazing map.

First, I noticed a series of passageways. So those were the ones located *behind* the walls? On the map they were outlined in gold. But I didn't see doors. How were we supposed to find a way in?

"Gee," Blix said sadly. "I wish I could read the map like you two. I'd give anything to be able to read this message here, along the bottom. . . ."

"What message along the bottom?" Rex panted.

"Wow! Good eyes, Blix!" I said, taking over. What looked like a bunch of meaningless curlicues at first were *words* hidden at the bottom. And the words spelled out something important in old-fashioned letters. Next to the words was a shape. Wait! It was a paw print! Was this message meant just for pups?

To Ye Who Find This Castle Map:
A golden paw is your way in.
One push and your quest will begin.
More golden paws on inner walls,
Hidden passage, secret halls.
Six more paws reveal the clue

Until great treasure comes in view.
Signed here by the King of Glimmer Rock,
Duff McDougal

"Wow!" I cried, wagging my tail. "This is the real deal! A treasure map with a riddle!"

"Look! Golden paws are shown on a lot of different places on the map," Blix noted. "Not just in the room with the *X*. They must mean something important, like the riddle says."

I was impressed with Blix. He couldn't read, but he sure had an eye for spotting important details. He was an especially valuable member of our puppy exploration team.

"Look! A golden paw is here on the map . . ." Blix said, "in the room we're in right now!"

"Really?" Rex asked. "I don't see a secret passage door anywhere."

"It wouldn't look like an ordinary entrance, remember?" I said. "King McDougal was craftier than that. Look for a golden paw print, I guess. . . ."

Rex sniffed wildly. "Maybe it's under one of the rugs?"

The library floor was covered with woolen rugs in all shapes and sizes. Together, we pushed and tugged at the edges of one large fringed red rug. Oh, how I hoped there would be a secret door in the floor!

Unfortunately, there was nothing here except for polished wooden planks.

"Let's look up instead of down," I suggested.

So we all looked up.

"Oooooh!" Blix cried. "Look at that ceiling! So pretty!"

The library ceiling was painted a beautiful dark blue with yellow stars. Some of the stars were grouped into outlines of animals. I spotted a lion and a crab.

No paw print.

"Those are constellations," I said. I knew this because Annie had shown them to me once in a book about space. She was always showing me things in books.

"Hey!" Rex cried out. "Is there a constellation in the shape of an arrow?"

"Wait! That arrow is pointing to something!" I cried.

"The bookshelf!" Blix said.

We scrambled over to it and stretched our paws up to try to reach the shelf.

Sadly, it was too high!

Rex had a good suggestion. "Maybe if I stood on Blix's back . . ."

Blix got down low so Rex could hop onto him. But the husky's fur was a little slippery, and Rex tumbled off.

"*Grrrrr!* Now what?" Rex growled.

"Try *my* back!" I said.

But my fur was slippery, too.

"Maybe we should just wake up Annie and James," Blix whispered. "They'll know what to do, right?"

"Oh," I sighed. I didn't want to wake them. I wanted this adventure for ourselves.

Rex felt the same as me. "We can't wake the princess and prince!" he yelped. "We have to figure this out on our own. If we wake them up, Annie will just take the map. And then James will send us to bed without our supper. *Rowf!* We'll get yelled at for tearing up the book from the king's library, and we won't get to go on an adventure, and then—"

"Hold on!" I said, interrupting Rex's panic attack. "I think I know a way to reach the bookshelf *without* their help."

"Woo-hoo! You do?" Rex cried. "How?"

Across the room was a wooden ladder attached

to a metal rod that wrapped around the entire library. I went over to the ladder. With my nose, I nudged the ladder, and it slid over.

Slowly, I climbed up onto the ladder steps. My paws gripped the treads carefully. I didn't want to slip and fall. When I reached the top, I touched the uppermost shelf with one paw. I expected some sort of enchanted lever to open and send me spinning down a chute.

But nothing happened.

"Try again!" Blix cried out enthusiastically.

I pressed and nothing happened again!

"This isn't working," I moaned.

"Try pressing the books instead of the shelf," Blix cried. "Wait! Look at that book on the very end! It has a golden paw print on its side! I nearly missed it!"

A golden paw print?

I remembered the line from the riddle on the map:

A golden paw is your way in.

One push and your quest will begin.

I glanced back down at the bottom of the ladder. Rex and Blix were doing the happy puppy dance.

"Push it! Push it!" they chanted.

So I did.

Chapter 3

Whew! The bookshelf was so dusty! I had to move sideways and use my tail to swat away an enormous cobweb. If this *was* the entrance to the secret passageway, no one had used it for a very long time.

"Nothing is happening," Rex barked up to me. He was standing on top of the map, checking it for more information. "What's going on?"

"We have to be patient," I called out. I scrambled back down the ladder to rejoin the other palace puppies—and wait.

Just as I reached the bottom step, we all heard a loud click.

Something creaked.

To our total surprise and delight, the entire bookshelf began to lurch forward.

It was opening! It worked! We poked our noses into the open space.

"So dark," Rex said.

"And damp," Blix added.

Palace puppies knew most things by smell. So we entered this secret passageway with a super sniff.

"Hmmmm," Rex said. "It smells like—"

"Cookies," Blix blurted out.

"Cookies?" Rex drooled.

"Why would a hidden passageway smell like cookies?" I asked.

We stepped into the darkness. The scent of good food made even the shyest of puppies do just about anything. As we moved inside, the bookcase shut behind us.

"Oh, no! The door closed! It's really dark!" Rex said. "I dropped the map!" He had been carrying it in his mouth.

"Hey," I whispered. "Check the walls. Maybe there's a light switch."

"A light switch? No way!" Rex said. "There can't be electricity in this part of the castle!"

Just then, Blix let out a yelp. "Over here!"

It took my eyes a moment to adjust to the darkness. When I finally saw more clearly, I spotted Blix nudging an old wooden crate with his snout. He pushed it closer to the wall.

"There *is* a switch!" Blix announced. "Look!"

"Hold on!" Rex barked. "I remember Prince James talking once about how the king and queen's family updated the castle years and years ago. They put in newfangled kitchens and heaters and *lights*! Of course! That explains the switch. They must have put lights in the passageways, too."

Blix leaped up onto the crate and, spinning around, used his strong tail to turn on the switch. As he did so, a line of gold lights flickered on along the passage walls.

"Wow!" We all gasped at the same time.

Up ahead, the passageway glowed. As we stepped forward, we appeared to glow, too—especially my goldendoodle fur.

"Now, *this* is magical," I said.

Blix's tail was wagging fast. "Being an inside dog is more fun than I thought!" he said.

"What are we waiting for?" Rex said. "Let's

go! I have the map and the *X* awaits!"

We ran through the passageway so quickly we nearly missed something enormous rising up out of the floor. . . .

Whoa!

Rex, Blix, and I screeched to a halt.

"Where did *that* come from?" I cried.

In the middle of the hall, a twisting staircase rose through the ceiling and disappeared through the floor. The stairs curled like a vine. It looked a lot like the spiral staircase inside Annie's oversize dollhouse. Which way would we go?

"We should go up, of course. To the secret tower!" Blix said.

"Or down!" Rex said.

"Map check!" I suggested.

Which way was the *right* way to go? There were quite a few choices. If we went up, the passageway twisted in several directions. If we went down, there was only one place to go. The lower level of the map was marked: DUNGEON.

Gulp.

Even Rex, who was the king of brave, was a little nervous about the prospect of a dungeon. We couldn't help thinking of the palace legends about former pups who had vanished there and never been seen again.

"M-m-maybe we should just go up," Rex stammered.

I nodded. "We can always come back the way we came in, right?"

"Besides," Rex said, reading the map some more, "there's a golden paw print going *up* the stairs. That looks right."

"Good call," I said.

"Race ya!" Rex said. Without missing a beat, he scooted up the staircase with the map.

I, of course, chased right after him. I never refused a race with Rex. Well, not usually, anyway.

Rex and I were almost at the top when I called back behind me, "BLIX!"

But I got no answer. That was when I realized that Rex and I were a party of two instead of three. I cried out. "Wait! Blix isn't with us!"

Quickly I turned around on the staircase.

"Blix, are you down there?" I asked in the dark. I heard a low whimper.

"Blix got left behind! I'm going back down to get him!" I yelped to Rex, and scooted down the stairs.

By the time I got to my husky friend Blix, he was shaking like a leaf.

"I'm so sorry!" I blurted out.

"Oh, don't be sorry!" Blix said, quivering. "The truth is I can't read the map like you two. Before I understood what you saw, you had already *gone*. I knew I should have raced after you. But I got confused."

"Oh, Blix, I won't ever leave you alone again. I promise," I said.

"I don't know," Blix said. "Maybe I'm not cut out for this adventurous castle life. . . ."

"Nonsense!" I cooed. "You are more adventurous than Rex and me put together! When we met at the Winter Palace, you and Rex had so much fun! You were *born* for adventure, Blix!"

"Even if that's true," Blix said quietly, "I'm just missing Mama and Axel and Chase. And I just can't shake this feeling. . . ."

Aha! It was the first time since he'd come home with us that Blix had admitted how he was *really* feeling. "Homesick?" I said. "I bet a treasure hunt will take your mind off things!" I suggested.

"You know, for an inside dog," Blix said, "you're really smart about outside dogs."

"Hmmmm," I said, chuckling. "I think I know what you mean."

"You think I'm brave"—Blix cocked his head to one side—"even when I don't feel so brave."

"Well, we all feel scared sometimes," I said to Blix. "And Annie and James told us a long time ago that whenever we get even the littlest bit scared, we need to keep our snouts held high. We need to remember that we're royalty."

Blix stood up a little taller and puffed out his furry chest.

"Gee, it's tough being the baby at the palace, isn't it?" I said.

"I'm *not* the baby." Blix flicked his ears. "Princess Rose is, remember?"

We both chuckled.

All at once, a doggy voice bellowed, "WE DON'T HAVE ALL DAAAAAAAY! ARE YOU COMING, OR WHAT?"

I looked at Blix. He looked at me.

"COMING OR WHAT!" we suddenly called back in unison, laughing.

When we reached the top of the stairs, Rex greeted us with an impatient growl.

"Let's go! Let's go!" he said, shaking the map in

his teeth. He led us under one of the brass lights attached to the wall. The three of us got a closer look at the map.

We checked out exactly *where* to find the next golden paw print.

According to my calculations, it should be located through an arched doorway. . . .

Aha! There! I see the arch!

We chased one another into a large, open space that had dim lights on the walls. There were tiles with designs like flowers and suns.

Who knew there were so many secret places to visit deep inside this castle?

My heart thrummed. It was like being told the best secret *ever*.

Grrrrrrrrrrrrrrrrrrrrumble.

"Whoa! Was that your tummy, Sunny?" Rex barked. He burst into a fit of giggles.

"Hey, quit laughing," I said. "I'm just getting hungry."

"I'm hungry, too," Blix confessed.

"Hungry? How can you two even think of food at a time like this?" Rex barked. "There's no time to waste! Somewhere, a treasure is waiting for us to find it!"

"Chill out," I cried.

Normally, *Rex* was the pesky, hungry, playful beagle who could focus only on food. But not today! Today, Rex was focused on something else: treasure.

Whoooooooooooooooosh!

"Hey! What was that?" we all said, jumping back from the map at the same exact time.

Rex stuck his nose into the air. "Wind?"

Whoooooooooooooooosh!

"Feels like wind," I remarked. The fur on my ears stood on end. Was it wind or was someone— or something—here with us? What was going on?

All at once, the room went pitch black. *"AAAAAAAAAAAAAAAAAAAAAAAAAH!"* We screamed and piled on top of one another in the darkness.

Chapter 4

Now, I consider myself to be pretty brave as far as royal goldendoodles go, but in that moment, when everything got so, so dark, I thought I was done for.

No one said a word for the longest time.

We stayed in that strange huddle, shivering with fear.

"Okay!" Blix said, moving out of the huddle. "Let's check out where that wind came from."

"Do we have to?" Rex asked nervously.

"Of course!" Blix said. "I hear something."

"Something?" I barked. "That's probably just Rex's teeth chattering."

"No! Wait!" Blix cried. "I hear something else."

I wanted to look deep into Blix's blue eyes. Their shimmer always calmed me down at times like this. But who could see anything in this darkness? I nuzzled Blix. He was making me a little nervous.

Squeak.

"Sunny?" Rex jumped. "Was that you?"

"Not me," I said.

"Shhhhhh," Blix said.

Squeak, squeak.

"Look!" Blix cried.

There in the dark near us were two teeny glowing eyes. They were much smaller than puppy eyes. And they were moving toward us.

"Who goes there?" I asked.

"Who goes there yourself?" the squeaky stranger said.

Before I could offer a reply, a light shone in the room. I found myself face to face with a McDougal Palace *mouse.* He wore a teeny helmet with a bright headlamp on it.

"Where did *you* come from?" I barked.

"Where did *you* come from?" the mouse asked back. "This is *my* house."

He didn't seem frightened at all, even though Blix, Rex, and I were each ten times his size.

"We're lost!" Rex cried. He was one shaky beagle.

"We're not lost," Blix said, holding up the map.

"We're just . . . exploring," I added.

"Trespassing is more like it," the mouse said.

Blix moved toward the light, and the mouse jumped backward.

"One more move and you'll be sorry!" the mouse shrieked.

"Hey!" Blix stopped short, tail wagging. "We don't want to hurt you," he said.

"We're happy to meet someone inside the secret palace passageways," I added. "We were just trying to find our way when there was this whoosh of wind and the lights went out."

"A whoosh? That must be the castle cooling-system vents," the mouse explained. "When the vents kick on, sometimes the electricity shuts down. The vents were fixed a few years back, but sometimes they don't work right. Although it feels like wind is blowing here, I'm afraid there's been no outside air in this part of the palace for centuries."

"You know so much about this place. Who *are* you?" I asked meekly.

"Sir Michael, the Palace Mouse," the mouse squeaked in a very royal tone of voice, bowing in

front of us. He removed his headlamp.

I giggled. A proper palace mouse! How was it that I had never run in to him before this?

"Do you live here alone?" Blix asked.

Sir Michael shook his head so hard his whiskers quivered. "Alone? Hardly!"

With that pronouncement, a cluster of other mice appeared. There were mice of all sorts: fat mice, short mice, bearded mice, fancy mice, black mice, gray mice, and lots of teeny-tiny white mice with squinty pink eyes. One of the mommy mice must have just had a litter of new babies. The mice came from all corners of the strange stone room. There must have been a hundred mice or more.

This chamber was different from some of the other rooms in the palace. It almost seemed as if it shouldn't have been a room at all. The

floor felt cold and damp on my paws.

I would have been truly scared if the mice weren't so nice.

Sir Michael properly introduced us to each and every mouse in the room, and I promptly forgot all their names. He explained how their mouse clan had been living a dandy life inside the walls of the castle for as long as his family could remember. They had run into real trouble only once, when the mice decided to go exploring and found themselves lost inside the main part of the castle with no way back to their home.

He explained how two very large women in gray dresses (I guessed maybe Nanny Sarah and Nanny Fran) had chased him and all the mice with brooms. And how the women had sent the castle cat to hunt for them! The cat was clever enough to find his way into the secret passageways. Unfortunately, the cat had captured many mice. That made me so sad.

Sir Michael held his teeny mouse paw over his chest. "We miss those mice each day."

Thankfully, Sir Michael reported, the bad cat had left the palace a few years later. He'd gone to live in another of the royal residences.

"That bad cat makes me think of Fitzsimmons," I muttered. He was the cat we'd met at the Winter Palace, where Blix used to live.

Blix stuck out his tongue and made a face. "Don't remind me of Fitz!"

Sir Michael squeaked in horror. "Just the mention of any cat makes me shudder!"

"There must be some good cats in the kingdom!" I said. One day, I vowed, I would find one.

Rex spread out the map to show Sir Michael where we'd been and where we wanted to go inside the palace walls.

"Aah!" Sir Michael gasped. "The map!"

The other mice gathered around. Excited squeaks filled the room.

"Have you seen this map before?" I asked.

He shook his head. "I've heard rumors of

this incredible map, but I have never seen it."

"We are trying to get up to the top," Rex explained, indicating the unnamed room marked with the *X*.

"Oh!" Michael said. "The secret tower!"

I glanced at Rex and Blix. A secret tower sounded so cool!

"But you must know," Sir Michael went on, "that the path to the top is not as simple as it seems."

"Isn't there an up staircase?" I asked. I pointed to a doorway on the other side of the room. "That would make sense."

"No." The mouse shook his whiskers at us again. "To go up, you must go down."

"Down, like . . . to the *dungeon*?" Blix asked.

"I don't understand," I said.

"I know it seems odd." Sir Michael nodded gravely. "But I think this might have been a trick King Duff played on his children. We've been living in these secret passages for a century. That's how it always works, even for creatures as small as us."

Sir Michael's whiskers twitched, and a smile stretched across his face. "I have something that may help you," he said. A pair of mice skittered over with something and placed it in front of me. It was a slightly larger headlamp, just my size. I put it on and the light shone on the wall ahead of us.

We gasped.

It was another golden paw print. There was our next clue!

"*Ooooooooooh!*" we cried, and raced over to read it.

> Through the arch you'll see a stone.
> Push it over and be gone.
> Ground will open, shake, and slide.
> Down you go: a palace ride.

"*Stone*? Is King Duff kidding?" I looked around the room.

This entire *room* was made of stone!

"I know! I know!" Sir Michael cheered. "Remember, you must go through the arch to find what you seek. Look for one enormous stone. Good luck!"

"We can't thank you enough, Sir Michael the Mouse," I called out as we waved good-bye to everyone in the room.

Mice are nice.

Just like that, the mice disappeared back into the walls. With my headlamp from Sir Michael on, we were all set to continue the adventure.

Despite my beam of light, we felt like the darkness was going to swallow us up from all sides. We needed to rely on our sharpest puppy senses more than ever.

Slowly, Rex and Blix followed me through the arched door. But Sir Michael had been right: the stone was easy to find! I spotted it right away, and it was as big as Blix!

Beneath the stone was a crack.

Rex pounced right onto it.

Kkkkkkkkkkkkkkkkkkkkkkk . . .

All at once, the floor shifted and the large rock moved. We lost our balance and fell onto the slippery stone. But this was no ordinary stone. This was a slide!

"OOOOOOOOOOOOOOOOOOOOOH!" we all howled at the same time.

The slide twisted and turned, and I felt my puppy body slam into the edges as we went down.

My ears flopped like crazy. We were going fast. Thankfully, Rex still had the map, but my headlamp flew off!

After the long slide, we were dumped out onto another stone floor.

Ker-thunk.

No one said anything at first. We were all too stunned to speak.

"Wheeeeeeeee-ooooooo!" Rex cried. "That was fun!"

"Fun? No, it was not!" I cried. "I didn't think that thing would ever stop!"

"We were going so fast!" Blix wailed. Even brave Blix had been a little scared.

This new room was cold and dark, but not as dark as it had been up where we'd fallen from. I spotted the headlamp and put it back on. It still worked!

After a few seconds, our eyes adjusted to the light again. I helped Rex tuck the map into his collar.

I could make the walls out better now. These were stone, like the room where we'd met the mice.

I spotted an enormous black bug with too many legs. How I hated bugs! Yeeech!

Was this the dungeon? There wasn't any of the usual stuff I would have expected to see in a dungeon, which was surprising. No strange bolts or chains hanging from the stone walls. No skeletons of prisoners who'd been forgotten.

As we sniffed along the floor, Rex remarked, "This doesn't seem like a real dungeon, does it?"

Grrrrrrrrrrrrrrrrrrrumble.

I jumped. "What was *that*?" I cried.

"Rex!" Blix barked in the dark. "Was that your tummy?"

The hungry grumbles sounded a little like monsters lurking in the darkness.

The truth was, we were all hungry. It had been a long time since we'd left the fireplace and made our way through the bookcase in the library. We'd not only gotten lost—but we'd lost track of the time, too. Had Sir Michael the Mouse sent us down, down, down . . . to the wrong place? Would we ever eat again? Would we ever see Annie and James again?

"Hey!" Blix woofed. He sniffed at the air. "Do you smell that?"

Rex and I poked our noses into the air, too.

"Is that . . . cookies again?" Rex growled excitedly. His tummy growled, too.

I danced up on my back paws. "COOKIES! Like we smelled earlier!" I said.

"The smell is a lot stronger down here," Blix insisted. His nose bobbed up and down more like a bloodhound's than a husky's. What a true talent for sniffing! After all his time in the barn, this dog couldn't deny his working-dog roots.

I was on sniff overload myself. I detected not only cookies but sausage links and pan potatoes with onion and lemon and . . . *mmmmmm* . . . meat. Steak tips were my absolute favorite palace treat.

Someone was cooking. I guessed it was Chef Dilly!

"What time is it?" I asked.

Neither Rex nor Blix had any idea.

Grrrrrrrumble.

My stomach gave me the answer I was looking for. It was time to eat!

I drooled at the thought of the food we would find back in the palace with Chef Dilly: hamburger and salmon and croquettes and berry scones with clotted cream. Annie would sneak me some cream from her scones whenever she got the chance. I couldn't wait for that. And the cookies! We'd been smelling them everywhere we went during our adventure inside the palace walls. There was nothing like a sweet treat at McDougal Palace to fill a puppy's tummy. Chef Dilly made the crunchiest puppy cookies.

If our little puppy bodies were *this* hungry, we must have been away from the princess and prince for a very long time. They'd probably woken up a while ago. The fire had probably fizzled out in the library. Naps were done. And the king and queen were probably in the sitting room at the other end of the hall wondering: WHERE IN THE CASTLE ARE THOSE PALACE PUPPIES?

I didn't want them to think we'd run away. We needed to find a way back—now. But I also wanted to keep searching for clues. *What was a pup to do?*

"Look!" I yelped. "A light! Over on the wall in the corner! Do you see it?"

Rex, Blix, and I raced to the light. Another golden paw print shone on the wall. Hooray! The electricity was working fine here.

Just like that, we found another rhyme to

read. Someone had painted words on the wall:

You have to go down before you go up.
Move in a pulley sized for a pup.

So Sir Michael the Mouse had been right!

Annie and James had told us that funny story about secret tunnels and special rooms filled with treasure. But nothing had prepared us for *this*. We really were *inside* Annie's palace storybook.

As we read the riddle, I noticed something else. This wasn't an ordinary wall! The riddle was actually written on a tiny *door* cut out of the middle of the wall.

"A door? What's *that* for?" Rex asked.

"*A pulley sized for a pup*?" I said, repeating the second line of the rhyme.

"There's something inside!" Blix said.

"Listen!" Rex barked. "Do you hear voices?"

Yes! It sounded like mumbling at first, but then the sound got clearer. I thought I recognized Chef Dilly's voice! Did this door lead up to his palace kitchen? I scratched at the door with my paws. Much to my surprise, a latch clicked and the door opened.

"WOW!" Blix cried.

It looked like a small box, well lit from inside. Light poured out.

"Hop in!" I told the other two pups. I left the headlamp outside.

Rex seemed worried, but Blix nudged him inside.

After we all scrambled in, I tugged the little door shut behind us. It turned out that the light wasn't coming from inside at all. It was coming

from *above* the little box. There was a panel in the ceiling that let the light in.

"This is crazy," Rex said. "Does anyone else feel a little squished?"

Blix chuckled. "It's like being inside the chicken coops back at the barn. We weren't ever supposed to climb in. But sometimes, when we played hide-and-seek . . ."

I laughed. "Blix, you're funny!"

"What's *this*?" Rex asked, pointing to a chain that hung on the side of the box. I bit down on the end of the chain. All at once, with a jerk, we began to move.

UP?

Where were we headed now? I remembered what Sir Michael the Mouse had told us. The clue had said: *You have to go down before you go up.* We'd slid down to the dungeon. Now we were riding up!

My stomach grumbled again, and I couldn't figure out if this aching tummy was from hunger . . . or sheer excitement! I closed my eyes and held my breath. Light filled the space.

The smell of cookies was getting stronger— and so were the voices we'd heard before.

Chapter 5

The contraption we were riding in, of course, was the old dumbwaiter.

Boy, was it creaky and slow!

Annie had shown me this big moving box once. With the simple tug of a chain, food or supplies could be delivered to different floors in the castle. A little door in the center of Annie's bedroom wall opened right into the dumbwaiter. She'd let me sniff around, but I was not, under any conditions, allowed to open that doorway or ride inside it.

"Tooooo dangerous," Annie had said.

And here we were. . . .

Oh, dear.

I thought about where we had gone today.

We'd been in plenty of danger already, but this dumbwaiter was the riskiest thing we'd done. Annie would have had a fit if she'd known. My paws were shaking just thinking about it. Would the dumbwaiter really be strong enough to hold the three of us?

And what would Annie do to me when she found out I'd disobeyed her?

Voices echoed loudly now in the shaft around the dumbwaiter. They were much closer. I put my ear up to the wall.

"Princess Rose needs a bath again."

"First we need to feed her!"

"She's a proper mess!"

Wait. Could it be? Those voices were so familiar: the nannies, the butler, the chef. Based on what was being said, I guessed that the dumbwaiter had to be passing near the kitchen. Or at least it *sounded* like it was. It was so strange to hear private conversations. Then again, we pups were always eavesdropping on human conversations in the castle.

"We have to bake a cake for Princess Rose?" another voice complained. "Imagine that! A cake for a baby?"

It had to be Chef Dilly! We all knew his voice

very well. It's easy to remember the voice of the man in the castle who makes the most delicious treats.

"Well, the king does call Rose *baby-cakes*," another cook in the kitchen said.

We listened closely to more talk. One woman went on and on about Princess Rose's eating and sleeping and cooing in her carriage. Was that Nanny Sarah?

"Princess Rose has been crying all day!" Nanny Sarah said. "She woke up with a start and wouldn't go back to sleep on her own. That thunderbolt just about did it, too. I've been sitting in the rocking chair with her for more than an hour!"

Quickly, my mind raced back to the booming noise we'd heard in the library. That was when our treasure hunt had begun. Poor Rose had woken up! Time had passed quickly while we explored inside these castle walls.

"Sounds like Rose needs us," Blix whispered to me. "Just like you told me: everything's better with a puppy close by."

I nuzzled Blix with my snout. "Not scary anymore when we're in this together, is it?" I asked. "But you're right. We should get back."

"Ummm," Rex looked around the dumbwaiter. "How exactly are we supposed to get back . . . from this?" He wiggled around, as impatient as ever.

"Shhhhh!" I cautioned. "Rex, you're rocking the dumbwaiter. . . ."

But Rex kept right on wiggling. He was getting way too fidgety for this small space.

"Rex! Hold still!" Blix whispered.

"*ROWOOOOOOO!*" Rex howled.

The dumbwaiter came to a stop.

"Rex," I whispered forcefully. "Now look at what you did! *Rowf!*"

Without realizing it, I'd barked, loudly.

Oh, no.

Someone heard me, of course.

"Was that a puppy barking?" one of the nannies asked.

Rex stopped moving. Blix stopped moving. I stopped moving. We all bit our tongues. We shut our snouts! I don't think the three of us had ever been that quiet.

"Yes, I definitely heard a dog bark," an unfamiliar voice said.

Try not to breathe, I told myself.

"But that's impossible!" the voice went on. "The

puppies are in the library with Annie and James. They all fell asleep by the fire."

Whew. They thought we were still in the library. That was good news.

"Wait a minute!" Nanny Sarah cried out. "I didn't see the pups in there when I went to check on the children. Have any of you seen them around the castle halls?"

"Those hounds are probably up to no good somewhere. . . ." Chef Dilly snorted.

We're not hounds! I thought. *I'm a goldendoodle!*

Rex snickered. "Well, he got the up-to-no-good part right. . . ."

"Shhh!" I cautioned Rex. "We don't want them to know we're inside this thing. . . ."

A nervous look crossed Blix's face. "We can't get caught. Please, Sunny," he begged. "If I get into trouble, I could be sent back to the Winter Palace!"

"Don't worry," Rex said. "James would never send you away."

"Neither would Annie," I said.

"NEVER," Rex and I said at the same time.

The dumbwaiter was getting a little stuffy now. Why had it stopped moving? Were we stuck? Thankfully, a moment later it lurched again, moving slower than before. But at least it was moving again!

Rex arched his beagle brows. "I guess that wasn't our final stop."

"You know, I like treasure hunts." I laughed. "But I'm not so sure I like dumbwaiters."

"I don't think they like you, either," said Blix.

"Speaking of treasure," I went on, "do you think the treasure in the room with the *X* will be shiny or golden or squeaky?"

"Squeaky like Sir Michael the Mouse?" Rex cracked.

I laughed. "Exactly."

All at once, the dumbwaiter stopped cold again. Blix sniffed around the door.

"I think we can get out here," he said.

"That was some ride," Rex said. "I want to do it all over again."

"No way!" I said. "Get out! GET OUT!"

I nudged Rex toward the little door.

Of course, getting out was easier said than done. We had to wiggle around, push open the door, come out of the dumbwaiter, land on the dusty floor, check the map *again* . . .

WHEW!

Thin shafts of light streamed up through the floorboards around us.

"So where are we *now?*" Blix asked. "In the room with the *X?*"

We looked down, and it was easy to guess our location by looking through the floorboards. We were now just *above* a pantry. I watched servants move back and forth carrying bags and trays and all sorts of goodies. They were talking some more.

"Come! Come! Chefs, we need to prepare dinner for the castle!"

I spotted a roast beef with some kind of roll, vegetables glazed with something that made them glow, those pan potatoes and cookies we'd smelled earlier. Oh, those were delightful snickerdoodles!

Foooooooooood.

We looked at one another. All the hungry feelings came rushing back. I wasn't 100 percent sure what *all* those fun foods were, but I definitely knew *snickerdoodles.* Those were the favorite cookies of the palace! Yum! I hoped my tummy wouldn't grumble again and give our secret hiding place away.

Hey! I felt something on my paw. It was wet and super slimy. *Ewwwwww! Rex!*

"Sorry," Rex whispered, licking his lips.

Without realizing it, he'd drooled all over me. One particularly large drip of his drool slipped right past my paw and through the opening in the floorboards.

Splat!

Luckily, it landed on the pantry floor and not on a chef's head or in a batch of batter.

Another close call!

"Do you have the map?" I whispered to Rex. "We need to get moving."

With his teeth, Rex tugged the map from where he'd been holding it all along: tucked into his studded collar. It was too dark and shadowy to read here, so we moved up ahead, where there were a few bright lights.

My paws ached from running and climbing through those secret passageways, but I helped to stretch the map out and flatten down the bumpy parts.

The only thing that was keeping me going was the idea of treasure and food. It was time to get on to the next golden paw print and see if we could finish this journey through the palace passageways.

"Gee," Blix said with a wide grin. "Things are really looking up. . . ."

He placed his paw on the map. The spot was directly above us. We all glanced up.

There was another golden paw print over our heads on the ceiling—along with another part of a riddle painted on top.

That Duff McDougal had planted plenty of tricky clues. We had nearly missed looking up to find this one. Thank goodness for the golden paws on the map—and for Blix's keen eyes.

Climb the stairs with bones galore.
Take yourself up just one floor.
Closet walls reveal what's true:
Other secrets wait for you.

Not only was there a paw print with a message, but there was also a strap hanging down with a bone attached to the very end! I immediately tucked the map back in Rex's collar and told Blix to hop onto my back. Then I ordered Rex to climb on to Blix's back. If we piled high enough, we'd be able to reach the strap.

There was only one problem.

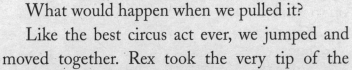

What would happen when we pulled it?

Like the best circus act ever, we jumped and moved together. Rex took the very tip of the strap in his mouth and tugged hard.

"Jump down!" I called out. We had to move quickly. The three of us leaped off one another's backs and scattered.

The golden paw came down from the ceiling. The strap had been attached to a hidden staircase. It dropped fast. Luckily, it didn't hit us—or the floor—too hard.

"Whoa," Rex said. "This secret-passage thing is getting better with every golden paw! A hidden staircase? Too cool!"

And this mysterious staircase was even more amazing than a plain old ordinary set of stairs. Each step of this staircase was carved and curved like a dog bone.

It was just like the clue had said: *Climb the stairs with bones galore.*

"Should we go up?" Blix said bravely.

"You bet!" I smiled broadly at our husky friend. "Lead the way!"

Chapter 6

The wooden "dog-bone" stairs felt smooth and slippery, so we went slowly. I don't think many pups or people had traveled up this way—at least not in the last century.

We had to be extra careful.

Duff McDougal had really set up a maze of twists and turns here. Our palace was better than the House of Mirrors at the beach or the silly amusement park in the middle of the city that Rex and I had visited once as baby pups.

When we got to the top of the stairs, Rex pulled the map from his collar and we eyed it once more. Blix gave it the real once-over—both Rex and I decided *he* was the one who was really good at spotting secret messages. That husky was *definitely* suited for life as an inside pooch in the royal palace. After I taught him how to read like humans, he would be unstoppable.

"Another golden paw print should be in this location on the map!" Blix cried. "That's what the riddle said: *Take yourself up just one floor!*"

But we didn't see another paw print here. *Hmmmmm.* I squinted and eyed our surroundings. We sniffed the floor for a familiar scent.

I stopped short. Someone was speaking again! But the voice wasn't Chef Dilly or the nannies. It wasn't coming from the pantry or kitchen. We were up a flight from those places. Who was it?

"We have to be on the floor with the bedrooms," Rex said, eyeing the map. I leaned over it with my headlamp so he could see.

Quietly, we crept toward the voices. And we listened closely.

It wasn't one person; it was two people, having a conversation.

And it wasn't just any two people!
IT WAS ANNIE AND JAMES!
We pressed our floppy ears (and sturdy ears, in

Blix's case) up to the wall. I heard our prince and princess talking softly inside one of the rooms. I could just make out what they were saying.

"I can't believe I fell asleep reading that book," Annie said. "It was supposed to be a special day with the puppies, and now they've run off."

"They're probably just having a bit of fun!" James said.

KERBLOOOM!

We jumped back. *That* must have been another thunderbolt. It was storming outside again. I imagined poor Rose, restless in her crib. I hoped she was still asleep after that noise.

"Oh, Sunny!" Annie wailed. "What if the puppies went outside? What if they're in the rain? What if they're in trouble?"

"They're not in trouble," James said.

"Rex is ALWAYS in trouble!" Annie cried.

I shot Rex a look.

Rex giggled. "Annie's right."

"Poor Blix isn't familiar with this place," Annie said.

Blix snickered. "Now I am!"

"Oh, why would they run off like this?" Annie said. "James, those pups are getting too daring. I'm not sure we should have let them roam around so much. What if they're hurt?"

James didn't say anything for a moment. Sometimes he had no argument for his sister. After all, Annie was usually right about these things. And James didn't seem especially bothered by his troublesome pup. But then, James *did* speak, and he said the perfect thing. Sometimes he's such a wise prince.

"Look, Annie, I know Rex is trouble," James said. "And I'm usually in trouble, too. But I think we need to trust the puppies more when they do things. They're smart. They're fun. And they look out for one another. I'm sure that—"

"*HOOOOOOOOOOOOWWWWWWWWWL!*"

Huh? I turned to Rex. He'd let out the loudest howl I'd ever heard.

"Rex?" James cried. "Is that you?"

"Scratch at the wall!" I said to Rex and Blix. "They can hear us!"

We started scratching and barking madly.

From the other side of the wall, Annie and James banged back.

"How did you puppies get in there?" James called out.

"*ROWF!*" Rex answered.

"Sunny, are you there, too?" Annie asked. "Quick! James! There is something behind this panel in my closet!"

"*WOOOOOF!*"

"Is Blix there, too?" James asked.

"*WWWWAAAAAOOOOOO!*"

"All three puppies are safe! Good!" Annie cried. She sounded so happy, and that made me happy. Now I wanted to see my princess again more than anything. The three of us began barking in a wild chorus of ruffs and growls.

"We'll get you out!" Annie cried, banging on the panel. "Keep making noise until I figure out how to open this. There must be a secret latch somewhere. . . . I always thought it was painted shut. . . ."

While she looked for some kind of latch, we barked even louder than before! Although this adventure had been a thrill, I was ready to leave the space inside the walls where we'd been roaming for so long. Now I imagined myself collapsing onto my soft, cushy doggy bed in Annie's room.

"Dad said our palace had secrets, but this

is ridiculous," James said, his voice muffled by the wall that was between us.

There were more whispers on the other side. Then I heard one much louder *BANG* and a *THUMP-THUMP* and finally a *CLICK-CLACK*. At last there was the sound of a lock being unlocked.

"You got it, James! Great job!" Annie said. I could hear every word. "How could I not have found this before today?"

"Hang on, puppies!" James cried. "We're coming in!"

"Coming in? Stand back!" I said.

From the other side, I heard rustling, shuffling, and pushing, and then all at once, the wall moved. I felt it. *Wow!* Princess Annie had always said half the palace doors led nowhere.

Now I knew differently.

Crrrrrrrrrrrrrrrrrrrreak.

Rex jumped back. "WAIT!" he barked. "What did the riddle say again? *Closet walls reveal what's true. . . .*"

Just like that, as the panel in front of us began to slide open, and light flooded into the space where we'd been standing, another panel slid open *behind* us!

Blix barked and howled. "This is way better than anything that ever happened back in the barn at the Winter Palace. Wow!"

And it was just as the riddle had said:

Other secrets wait for you.

The secret panel behind us, triggered by the panel from Annie's closet, revealed something astounding . . . something *paw-shaped*!

Whoa! Another golden paw print and riddle had been hidden there the entire time.

Paws inside the gallery,
You'll find one puppy holds the key.
Turn the key into a lock,
And go inside the puppy clock.

Before I could think about what the new riddle meant, Annie burst inside.

"SUNNY!" she cried. I leaped into her arms.

The other two puppies followed me through the open panel. Some clothes that were hanging up fell to the floor. Rex got his paws tangled up in one of Annie's scarves. Blix fell into a pile of

sweaters. It was a crazy reunion for all of us!

Being back in Annie's room felt so good. There was my comfy bed, right there in the corner by the huge picture window. *Aaaaaaaaah.*

"Rex! Blix! What on earth were you doing inside the palace walls?" James cried, grabbing them both. "I'm so glad you're okay."

Annie cradled me in her arms. I'd never enjoyed a hug from my princess more than right then. I felt so safe.

No matter how bold or brave I tried to be, I was always happy to be a puppy baby.

Annie smelled so good now, too, like flowery lilac soap. Me, on the other hand, I smelled like stinky cobwebs, dust, and—*eeeek!*—mice.

"I can't believe you have a secret door in your closet, Annie," James said. "I'm totally jealous."

"You probably have one, too," Annie said.

"Nope," James said. "I've checked a zillion times. And you have that dumbwaiter thing, too."

"Yeah, but I don't use it. Remember what Mom said about the dumbwaiter? A long time ago, one of the palace pets went inside it, and the whole thing crashed to the ground."

"Whoa!" James made a face. "Are you saying

that if the puppies had climbed into the dumbwaiter they might have been crushed into little hamburgers?"

"*RUFF! RUFF! RUFF!*" Blix and I gasped at the same time. "WE COULD HAVE BEEN *HURT*?"

"More like *splat*," Rex snickered.

"*Arowwww*," I growled at Rex playfully. Why couldn't he just *be quiet*?

As much as I loved seeing my princess again, I had to tell Annie about the other paw print and keep searching for the *X* on the map. How would I let her know about the clues?

Carefully, I nuzzled Annie's leg and panted to get her attention. *Over here!* I said to her with my eyes and tail.

Annie thought I wanted a snack! She reached into a drawer and grabbed a handful of emergency dog cookies. She kept a stash by the bed for nights when she gave me special treats. The three of us ate half a bag of the snacks in under ten seconds.

"You'd think I never feed you, pups," Annie said.

I moaned. Today that wasn't so far from the truth! Then I tried to direct her attention back to the closet and through the secret panel.

"Rowf! Rowf!" I barked, spinning in a circle.

Rex let out a whoop, too, to get James's attention. As he shook his body, the McDougal Palace map, circa 1780, signed by Duff McDougal himself, came untucked from his collar. Now it was time for James and Annie to see it.

"Whoa!" James blurted out when he picked up the map. "What's this?"

Annie's eyes bugged out. "Where did you get this? Rex, did you steal this from somewhere? Did you drag this out of some corner of the castle? Have you been hiding behind a sofa somewhere gnawing on it?"

Rex panted quietly. His tail slipped between his legs.

I didn't want *any* of us to get into trouble for ripping the book or going on our adventure. After all, we'd sort of *stolen* the map from the library earlier, hadn't we?

But we were too far along to stop our adventure now. In order to finish, we needed Annie and James to help us find the treasure.

"Puppies," Annie crossed her arms, addressing the three of us at once. "Do you three want to tell me what kind of trouble you've been making behind our backs? When we fell asleep in the library, just where did you three *really* go?"

I thought about the mice and the stone slide and the dumbwaiter and how wild things had been. If we couldn't explain *everything* about what we'd been doing, we could *show* her where we'd been. We could lead her to the newest riddle and have her and James solve its mystery!

Quickly, I barked a little bark, snatched the map out of Annie's hands, and dashed back toward the closet. Once she saw the paw print with the map, she would understand.

"SUNNY!" Annie called out. "Bad dog! Sunny! Come back! Where are you going? Give me the map!"

James yelled, "STOP!" and dived for me, but I darted from left to right and he didn't even manage to grab my tail.

This puppy wasn't stopping—not until Annie and James understood what we had to do and where we had to go from here.

Three pups, a princess, and a prince! We were all in this together.

Chapter 7

Finally everyone was back in the closet with me. I poked my snout behind the secret panel.

"Why are you going back there again?" Annie cried out.

I dropped the map under the paw print and barked. Rex, who had been rather quiet for a bit, let out a whooping noise. He and Blix howled in unison, actually. We were howling, "LOOK AT THE WALL AND THE MAP! NOW!"

"Shhhhh! Shhhhh!" James warned us dogs. "Nanny Sarah will hear you. So will Nanny Fran. Keep it down. We don't want them to see our secret door."

"Sunny! Rex! Blix!" Annie said. "I've never seen you act so sneaky! Stop this right now!"

The princess hardly ever raised her voice, but we puppies didn't budge.

"WHAT IS GOING ON HERE?" Annie cried. She sounded frustrated. Oh, how I hated it when my princess was upset.

But she didn't have anything to worry about.

The three of us pups knew what we were doing. James figured that out.

"Annie, hold on! Look!" he cried. "I think maybe the puppies are trying to show us something on the inside of the wall! It looks like a picture . . . and words!"

I breathed a deep sigh of relief. At last! Annie and James saw it. They could help us figure out the clue about the gallery! With their help we'd find the *X* for treasure for sure!

"A paw print? Who wrote something in here?" Annie said. "Has this been on the inside of my wall the whole time?"

"Ooooh, it's a riddle! I love riddles," James said. "Especially riddles inside a secret passageway! This is like a scene from a movie!"

I could see the thoughts pinging around inside

the prince and princess's heads as they looked from the wall to us and back again. Everything was beginning to come together.

I nudged the map toward Annie. She finally picked it up and took a close look.

Excitedly, I poked my snout at the area on the map that showed this paw print. I had to make her see the connection.

Annie looked at the map and then back up at the secret wall.

At last she read the riddle aloud.

Paws inside the gallery,
You'll find one puppy holds the key.

Annie scratched her chin. "Key? What is this? What does it mean? The gallery? Hmmmm. Are we supposed to go there? Wait. Is this some kind of treasure map?"

"ROOOOOOWWWWOOOO!"

The three of us began howling again.

Rex jumped onto James and licked his hands furiously.

"Stop!" James laughed. "Sis, I think this riddle is telling us where to go," he said.

Yes! At last! Blix, Rex, and I got up on our hind paws and formed a puppy conga line. We did our best celebration dance *ever*. They had figured it out!

"*Gallery* must be the portrait gallery," James mumbled.

Aha! I'd forgotten all about the portrait gallery in the main part of the castle. So, not all of the paw print clues were hidden inside the walls? That Duff McDougal was one crafty king.

There was no time to waste!

We scampered away from Annie's upstairs bedroom, past James's room, and down the staircase with the beautiful banister. Running down the main stairway always made me feel like a royal puppy more than anything, but today I wasn't stopping to revel in my royalness. Today I was a pup on a mission!

"To the gallery!" James cried. Rex and Blix followed right behind us.

Annie was waving the map in the air. "Wait for me!" she cried.

We flew into the passageway.

This gallery had always been such a quiet and peaceful place to wander. I loved being here, looking at the portraits of all my ancestors. Now that I'd traveled *inside* the castle walls, I felt a stronger connection to the history of the place than ever before.

There were portraits of dogs who had belonged to kings and queens, painted in their fine gardens next to rosebushes and fiery blooms. There were all sorts of dog breeds I didn't even know. Dogs were clustered together at parties and hunting trips. There were dogs in robes, dressed to look like kings themselves. There were dogs in the water, dogs with bones, dogs with books. I loved looking at the different-colored fur and stripes and spots. So many beautiful palace puppies!

"You'll find one puppy holds the key," Annie recited aloud as we walked around. The answer to this riddle was around here.

But where?

Now she and James were getting excited by the treasure hunt, too. I loved having them be a part of this quest. Although it was fun roaming around earlier with my puppy friends, it was even better to share this experience with our prince and princess.

Unfortunately, the more we looked for a puppy holding a key, the less sure I was that we'd find one.

There were no keys—not a one!—in any of the canvases.

After a few quiet and searching moments, Blix leaned in to me.

"Maybe the *key* wasn't actually being held by a puppy," Blix said to me. "Maybe it wasn't actually in the art? Maybe the key in question was somewhere else, like on a flowerpot? Or maybe on a frame?"

Rex and I sniffed around each portrait carefully. Blix really had terrific puppy sense.

"Ruff! Ruff! Ruff!" I barked softly, and got Annie's attention.

In front of me, in one of the many portraits of Duff McDougal himself posing with one of his enormous sheepdogs, there it was.

A key in the frame!

We could all see that there was an overall design to the frame showing dogs with keys in all shapes and sizes around their necks and in their mouths. But one dog with a key appeared to be raised ever so slightly from the surface of the frame. Annie touched that key gently.

It shifted! It came loose!

Annie held the key up to one of the clean white lights above the portrait. It was a dark walnut color

on one side—the side that had been showing on the frame. But on the opposite side, it sparkled. On top of the key was the imprint of something we'd been seeing all over the palace all day: a perfect golden paw print. Wow! This time the paw print was on an actual object and not just on the wall. What did *that* mean?

King Duff was too cool.

Annie and James jumped up and down as if they were on some kind of imaginary trampoline. They whispered back and forth about whether they should tell the king and queen about the map and the key. Or maybe Nanny Sarah should know?

No!

One word to a grown-up in the castle could mean a halt to our quest.

Luckily, Annie and James didn't want to tell them what was going on, either. No one would breathe a word. This was a secret the five of us would share. We would decipher the next part of the golden paw print clue together.

Turn the key into a lock,
And go inside the puppy clock.

At the very end of the portrait gallery, between the huge potted plants and antique tables, there was an old clock. We hustled over to see it up close.

"This thing is amazing!" James said as we gazed up at the clock face. On the front of the clock was a group of dancing puppies. The clock hands were thin dog bones going around in perfect time. The pendulum for the grandfather-clock body was carved in the shape of a paw print. This *had* to be the right place.

"Where can we fit a key?" Annie asked nervously.

We all looked (and some of us sniffed) around the body of the clock.

On the base, there appeared to be a little door. But it was dog-size, not people-size.

Annie put the key into the keyhole anyway.

It clicked.

We held our breath as she turned the key, but what happened next surprised us all more than we could have imagined.

The small door was actually a trick! The *entire* side of the clock opened wide when Annie inserted the key into the lock.

"Whoa!" James said. "I thought it was just a teeny door, but look! We can all fit inside."

Annie leaned in to look. "Wow! It's more than a door! There's a staircase!"

"Stairs inside the clock?" James said. "Hmmmm. Maybe it goes up to a secret tower?"

"There's no such thing as a secret tower in this castle!" Annie said. "Daddy told us that a long time ago."

"But what about the picture on the front of the McDougal Palace book?" James asked. "There's a light on in that picture!"

"Oh, James! Daddy told us that's just made-up," Annie replied. "The tower on the top of this castle is nothing more than a bunch of stones and dust. You know that."

I barked and shook the map in James's face as if to say, *Take this! Take this! There's a big* X *in that tower!* The room with the *X* that was not labeled had to be the *secret tower.* We'd found the treasure for sure!

James snatched the map from me. "Check out the map, sis," James argued, pointing out the secret tower. "It shows something up there. . . ."

"This isn't some kind of special-effects movie,

James," Annie said. "Maps don't lead to treasure chests. Puppies don't crack codes."

James threw up his arms. "Well, let's go and see for sure."

"Fine!" Annie said. She pulled out a small flashlight from her pocket and clicked it on. When we'd been in the bedroom, she'd grabbed the light, some extra cookies, and a few other things, too. My princess tries to be prepared for anything. I think she likes a good adventure as much as we puppies do.

One by one, we went inside the puppy clock.

Chapter 8

These were some steep stairs.

It was hard to believe we were climbing up *inside* a grandfather clock. We heard it ticking loudly as we went up. Then the ticking stopped. We were on another staircase in the castle walls.

"This is amazing!" James said, waving the map. "I feel like a pirate or a spy or—"

"An explorer!" Annie said. She moved to the front to lead the way.

We puppies were all panting. I think we'd climbed enough stairs that day to last us a lifetime.

"What do you think we'll find at the top of the tower?" James asked. "Besides the light and the treasure and a whole lot of—"

"*ROOOOOOWF!*" Rex barked. It sent a loud echo up and down the staircase.

James nearly lost his balance.

"James!" Annie scolded. "Can we focus, please?"

Annie's flashlight beam danced in front of us as we continued up and up. "I can't believe we made it," I whispered to the other pups. "*X* marks the spot—at last!"

"We're almost at the top!" Annie said—softly, though, so there wouldn't be another loud echo.

She stopped briefly on the stairs and asked James to hand her the map. James spread it out as Annie focused the light on the top part.

MCDOUGAL PALACE, EST. 1780

She moved the light down a little. There was the outline of the stairs we were now climbing, but the pencil or pen on the map was very light. I think we would have missed this part of the journey if Annie and James hadn't led us to the portrait gallery.

Finding treasure really was all about teamwork, wasn't it?

"So we stop here," Annie muttered softly. "Behind a door at the top, we will find the exact place that shows the *X* on the map. Is this the place you want to find, puppies?"

"ROWF!" we barked softly, trying not to make another echo.

"Wait!" James yelled. "Before the treasure is revealed, I just would like to thank my favorite puppies for finding the best way EVER to spend a rainy day in the castle. I knew there was a reason I loved you pups."

I wagged my tail. Sometimes he was a little wild, but James wasn't *always* as annoying as Annie made him out to be. He believed in us today. He *loved* us.

The top was very close now. Annie took a deep breath. Slowly, she turned a doorknob at the top of the stairs. The door swung open and we raced in.

"WHOA!" we all barked.

"What is *this*?" James cried out.

We were in another room—a room no one ever talked about. It was a tower room.

Unfortunately, this tower room was nothing more than stones and dust. Just like Annie had said. My heart sank.

Annie shrugged. "I'm sorry, James. I told you that the legend of treasure and a secret tower was just a fairy tale. Sometimes a tower is just a tower . . . dust and all. . . ."

I raced around and chased my tail in frustration. This just couldn't be! After everything we'd been doing all day, it led us on a wild-goose chase to *here*? Impossible!

Rex and Blix just stood there hanging their heads. They didn't even know what to say. And for Rex, the chatterbox beagle, that was a pretty big deal.

Annie looked around the place.

"Stones and dust," she said. "I wish it had been more. I want to believe in treasure maps just like you do, Sunny."

Annie bent down and stroked my soft golden ears.

"After we get back downstairs, we'll have Chef Dilly give you some big plates of yummy dinner."

I rubbed up against Annie's leg. It was more of a cat move than a puppy move, but it got me what I wanted most at that moment: her attention. Annie scratched under my collar.

"I really am sorry, Sunny," she went on. "I know how disappointed you are. I know you were looking forward to finding something incredible up here."

Squeak.

Hey! I pricked up my ears.

"Did you hear that?" Blix barked at me.

Rex heard it, too.

Sir Michael the Mouse?

All at once, the tower was filled with the sounds of squeaks.

Annie let out a scream. So did James.

"MICE!" they squealed.

I barked and pretended to chase the mice around the room. Annie and James leaped up onto a stone bench at the side of the room.

Of course, I didn't want to chase Michael anywhere. "What are you doing here?" I asked him on the sly.

He bowed. "I'm sorry to catch you and your princess like this," Sir Michael said. "But the mice and I wanted to see that you made it to the tower."

"We did. We went down like you said and then up again. But I guess there was no treasure to be found."

Annie was waving her arms in the air frantically. "Mice! Mice! Help!"

"Yikes!" James said.

While Annie and James fussed and jumped around, I quickly pulled Sir Michael over to the side. Blix and Rex chased the other mice in circles so it *looked* like they were getting rid of the mice. Annie and James had no idea we were all pals. We wanted to keep Sir Michael's castle secret for a little while longer. The princess and I have an understanding, but she doesn't know that I can actually talk, and she definitely doesn't know that I hang out with other animals.

"I'm so glad to see you again," I whispered, relieved, to Sir Michael.

"Me, too!" Sir Michael cried. "We just came by to help. When we go, check the wall above our hole. There's your stone to turn this time."

"ROWF!" I barked. "Come and visit us in the palace sometime when no one will see you."

"Until we meet again!" Sir Michael called to me with a bow.

The mice scattered. "Until we meet again!" they said. Their whiskers twitched madly.

I jumped onto the stone bench. It gave us a good view through these little windows between rows of stones that looked out onto the McDougal Palace property.

I'd never seen the view from the palace like this. It was extraordinary to see the gardens and the topiaries shaped like puppies from up so high, especially in the midst of such a rainstorm. Everything was blowing and swaying!

But the outdoors wasn't what I needed to see most. I wanted a view of where the mice were scampering off to. Aha! The mice got into a single-file line and disappeared into a shadowy hole in the stone wall.

"Oh, thank goodness, the mice are gone," Annie said. "I'm sorry, Sunny. I don't think there's any treasure." She jumped off the bench. "Maybe Duff McDougal really was just playing a trick on us all."

I wagged my tail.

"NO! LOOK! HE WAS NOT PLAYING A TRICK!" James blurted out.

"Huh?" Annie said.

"Duff McDougal was a genius! And Rex, you're a genius, too."

Rex sniffed his way over to that mouse hole in the wall. He poked a paw inside.

Had Sir Michael Mouse and his fellow mice led us to another clue?

We all made a beeline for the other side of the tower room and the stone wall where Rex stood. At first glance the wall ahead looked like all the other walls in the place. Upon closer inspection, however, there was something hidden right there in plain sight.

James brushed away dust from a large, odd-shaped stone. The stone was lighter than the other ones around it, too.

Annie gasped. "What is this?" she cried.

Underneath the dust on the stone was another paw print! This one wasn't golden, but there was a message inscribed in tiny letters around the paw print. It *was* another clue!

All we had to do was follow the instructions.

Annie read the new riddle aloud. Rex, Blix, and I put on our puppy thinking caps.

You've traveled down, you've traveled up,
You've almost found the treasure, pup.
Check this wall and find a gap:
A very special booby trap.

"Uh-oh," James said. "Booby trap?"
"That means be careful!" Annie said.

"So now do you think maybe there *is* treasure in the secret tower?" James asked.

Annie smiled. "Maybe you were right."

Rex, Blix, and I sniffed all over that tower wall for some kind of booby-trap gap. Finally, after a whole lot of sniffing, we found an enormous crack in one large, off-colored stone.

I barked at the crew, "Over here! Look!" Everyone ducked down to check out the crack—and where it led. Our tails were wagging so hard we kept knocking each other over. This. Was. It.

"Out of the way," Annie said as she leaned hard into the cracked stone. She knew how to trigger this new booby trap.

After what had happened with the clock downstairs, I expected the entire stone wall to open up wide, just like the bookcase had opened when this adventure began.

But this opening was actually much smaller. This one was perfectly pet-size!

Annie and James could fit; they just had to get down on their hands and knees and . . . SQUEEEEEEEEZE.

After a few moments, we'd wriggled through, stepped out from under a few stones, and walked

into a room that was a lot more than stones
and dust.

This annex was packed with treasure!

"It *is* real!" Annie gasped.

We immediately noticed that there
was one small window here, too, just
like the window that had been on

the book cover. Next to this window was a lamp. When it was on, it had to be the yellow light that appeared in the picture! The glass on the window was old and thick with dust, too.

The secret tower room, for all of its hype, was on the smallish side. But it had plenty of room to fit all of us. And what it lacked in size it more than made up for in contents.

This place had been treated with tender loving care years earlier. It felt like a time capsule. It was packed to the brim with objects from long ago and decorated with old-fashioned pictures and rugs.

This secret tower treasure *was* fit for a queen, or at least a princess. It was as golden and glittery in here as in other parts of the castle. Golden just like me! I noticed that the wallpaper shimmered. The chairs were encrusted with colorful jewels.

We had stumbled into a place that had not been visited by royal subjects, pups, or kittens for a century or more. The only ones who had come here were gray and squeaky, led by the honorable Sir Michael the Mouse.

Very carefully, we began to poke our snouts around the place.

Chapter 9

I tiptoed across the small room. Rex and Blix scurried behind me. Along the walls in the secret tower were boxes and bins in all shapes and sizes. There were three enormous chests, as well. Where to begin?

We eyed the first chest, a blue one, speckled with silver stars. On the top was just one word, painted in dark blue: MCDOUGAL. What was in this family chest? Was *this* the treasure chest we'd been reading about in those clues on the map all day long? Was this a treasure chest filled with coins and jewels and other kinds of riches?

No! It was a costume chest filled with capes and shawls!

"I love dress-up!" I declared as I lurched forward to get whatever was inside the chest. "This is filled with clothing that's perfect for puppies!"

Blix made a funny face. "I've never really played dress-up before."

Rex snarled. "I have. Nanny Fran liked to dress me up when I was just a wee puppy. Don't remind me. . . ."

"Oh, it's fun!" I squealed, wiggling a cape around my shoulders. It was just right for a goldendoodle, and it had a snap on the front that Annie did up for me so it wouldn't fall off. I passed two black capes and masks over to Blix and Rex. "Try them on!" I said.

Rex grumbled, but he let James model his cape. Blix dressed up, too.

Something happened when they wore those costumes. Something magical. Those two palace puppies began to dance and twirl around the place. They first acted like villains and then stepped up onto a stool and pretended to be superheroes on an ocean liner solving crimes of the sea!

I found a blue-green mermaid costume with scales and sequins sewn all over. I made up an adventure story about a castle under the sea with a secret chamber of fish and sharks and eels. It was the best dress-up fantasy ever!

"Hey!" Annie cried. She had dressed up, too, in a pink feathered hat. James was holding a bow-and-arrow set.

"Don't forget us," James said, aiming an arrow at Rex.

Rex let out a little howl and then fell to the ground, playing dead, with his paws up in the air.

Annie laughed. She reached into the clothes bin and pulled out a flowered dress. It was really too small for her, but she acted as if it fit. Annie grabbed my paws and pretended to dance with me.

Then she scooped me up so we could look out the side window. We stared down over the castle grounds.

A shoestring bolt of lightning streaked across the gray sky. Wow! There was so much to see, inside and out. The rain pelted the thick glass.

Annie found a latch on the window and opened it a tiny bit: just enough to let in a little bit of fresh air without getting us all wet.

Aaaaaah.

I took a deep breath. The air was cool and smelled like rain.

Meanwhile, Rex and Blix started dive-bombing the toys in the room. Every time one toy was taken out, another was flung through the air. And nothing was getting picked up.

I got back to playing myself. I peeled off my mermaid suit, tugging at the edges with my teeth but careful not to drool too much on it.

What other fun thing could I put on?

Blix showed me a big orange box chock-full of hats and crowns in all sizes. He'd already pulled on a jester hat with bells and was making a racket.

"Blix! Awesome!" James cried.

Many of the hats had convenient ear holes so they could fit on top of my puppy head.

Blix suggested that we try on every single hat, so we did. And of course Annie and James joined right in.

There were sailor caps, bowler hats, top hats, and more. My favorite hat was one with a funny propeller on the top. I let Blix poke it so it spun around and around.

The princess, the prince, and we puppies moved from one box to the next, from one activity to another.

At some point, Rex found a box with jacks and

a small ball made of tough canvas. And there was a clear case filled with glass marbles, too—hundreds of them! Rex bit open the top of the case. Uh-oh! Marbles plinked one by one by one onto the floor. They rolled into every corner of the room.

"Look out!" Annie cried, sidestepping the marbles.

We found all sorts of fun in there: a ringtoss game in a box marked QUOITS, a cup and ball with a stick painted to look like a giraffe, little drums with blue drumsticks, and much more.

After playing awhile, Annie took out our map and placed it on a small table in the center of the room. I took a good, long look. We'd traveled on so many of these marked paths over the past few hours.

"Did you puppies walk through the entire castle today?" Annie asked in disbelief.

Little did she know we'd done more than walk through the castle. We slid down to the dungeon! We rode up in the dumbwaiter! But I had to keep all that a secret. I didn't want Annie to worry anymore.

But I'd keep those secrets. I didn't want Annie to worry any more than she already had.

I'm not sure how long we were in the secret tower before I realized that we'd better hurry up and go. The king and queen were no doubt searching for all of us at this point. I'm sure Chef Dilly's delicious dinner was in the process of being prepared. Although Annie had given us all some more cookie snacks up here, I needed a real meal.

I marched over to nudge Annie so she'd know I was hungry, but she'd found a box of old books and letters. Annie held up one handwritten letter.

"Look," she said. "It's addressed to someone named Rose."

Rose! Like the princess!

Annie read the letter.

"My dearest Rose," she read. *"I must travel on the sea. I will so miss thee. Remember what I said. Always keep me in your head."*

More rhymes!

"This must have been written by King McDougal," Annie explained. "Long, long ago. I bet this room was made for the original Rose of the castle."

"Wow!" James said. He looked the letter over, too.

All this talk about Rose got me thinking. It had been a little while since we'd seen the palace baby.

We hadn't heard her cry since the lightning storm. I wondered how she was doing. Was she fast asleep in her crib? I bet she would have loved my mermaid costume. There were so many things up here that she could play with when she got a little bit bigger.

A set of tortoiseshell combs for her dolls when she got older?

A rhinestone collar? Of course, that was for a puppy, not a baby!

Some blocks with pictures instead of letters? Perhaps when she learned to sit up and play.

A chimpanzee on stilts that flipped over and around like he was doing a circus trick? Would Rose like *monkeys*?

Hmmmm. I needed to find something that Rose would love, something shiny or soft.

Many toys up here weren't exactly right for a sweet baby, but I was determined to find something. I shuffled through a second large chest that was black, with metal knobs on the side. It was beat-up looking, as if it had traveled on one too many train rides home.

"Pssst!" Blix whispered to me. "Are you looking for something special?"

I nodded. "Yes! For Rose! We said we'd find her

some kind of special toy while we did our treasure hunt, remember? We have to bring her back something!"

"There must be something here for a baby," Rex said. "If we get her the perfect toy, maybe she'll never cry again."

I laughed. "Or at least it will make her smile more." I sniffed around and around. Rex helped.

Then, at the very edge of the room, I saw something glimmer. Something shiny! Something GOLD!

I scooted over and dug it out of a pile of some fancy doll clothes. As I pulled on it, the gold object began to play music.

What was this special thing?

"Oooh, a mobile!" Annie cried. "That's really beautiful, Sunny!"

The mobile was golden, just like me, and just like all the paw prints we'd seen today! And it had teeny puppies dangling from it. There were six dogs in all, including a dachshund and a Dalmatian and a fluffy dog that looked a lot like a poodle. Each puppy on the mobile had been dipped in gold. When those pups caught the light, they shimmered.

"You can give this to Rose," Annie suggested. "It plays music, so Princess Rose will finally fall asleep."

Of course, Annie had no way of knowing that that had been my plan all along!

Rex dug around in the clothes, too. He wanted to find his own treasure. After a few dives into the pile, he came up with something shiny for Rose, too: a silver rattle!

"Wow," James cried. "You puppies really know how to find the loot."

These were perfect presents for Princess Rose.

I hopped up into Annie's lap, looking for a "good dog" or a pat, pat, pat on the head. She took the mobile from me carefully and gave me the praise I was looking for.

"You are so thoughtful, Sunny," Annie said. "That's why you're my dog." Then she smothered me with a big hug.

"And so are you!" James cried to Rex, taking the rattle from him.

Blix looked a little left out.

"Rowf!" I barked to him. "Why don't you get Rose a gift, too?"

Blix's eyes lit up. "Good idea!"

He dashed across the tower room and poked his nose into boxes and under a big chair. Quickly, he came up with a present of his own for the littlest princess. Blix found Rose a sweet, soft, pink blanket covered with embroidered roses! Not only that, but it had her name at the very top, stitched in a darker pink thread: ROSE.

"Today I learned to read a little bit," Blix whispered to me proudly. "Do you think the princess will like this?"

"Of course she will!" I said.

Blix brought it to Annie and pressed it into her lap.

"You're *all* good dogs!" Annie announced, and gave Blix a pat. "But now we'd better hurry back."

That was when we heard a loud clang.

"Now what was that?" Annie wondered aloud.

James stopped and listened closer.

"IT'S THE CLOCK!" he cried.

"Oh, no!" Annie cried. "Dinner with Mom and Dad! If we don't get back down into the main part of the castle, we're all going to be in big, big trouble."

All I had to hear was the word *dinner*.

We tidied up a little, but we knew we'd be back

in our secret tower again very soon. This was *our* place. Rex grabbed the treasure map in his teeth again and slid it under his collar.

On the way out, I noticed something we had not seen on the way in. It was framed on the lower part of the back of the door. I barked, and Annie read it aloud.

When you've had all your fun,
Remember this before you run:
Thy hunt is done, well done to thee.
Just put the map back carefully.

Chapter 10

Later that night, I, Sunny, the Palace Puppy, ate more helpings of dinner in my dog dish than I had ever eaten before. Rex and Blix ate a lot, too.

I never wanted to have such a hungry tummy again.

I went over the events of the day in my head, and I could not remember a time at the palace when I'd had so much adventure. I learned a lot about my family and the place where I live. Most important, Blix felt like a proper member of our clan. He told me so.

The story Annie read to us was what got the whole day started. I wondered how many more secrets there were inside our palace. Because now I wanted to explore them ALL!

After our enormous feast, the king and queen learned from Annie and James that we puppies had something special we wanted to share with the new baby.

They decided to throw a little celebration in Princess Rose's honor the very next afternoon. Annie told me that at the lunch, we could present Rose with her rattle, her mobile, and her perfect blanket.

In return, we were promised something special.

My mind raced at the thought of that.

The next afternoon, we were brought into the royal bath for some "pampering." That's what Annie called it. Rex still had the treasure map from the day before inside his collar. He put it under a sofa cushion for safekeeping before getting into the bath.

Nanny Sarah, who's in charge of the kids, and Nanny Fran, who's our "pet" nanny, both appeared, their arms filled with supplies: powder, soap, creams, brushes, combs, and even a pretty pink barrette to clip back the longest locks atop my head.

Everything smelled delicious. Of course, since

it *smelled* good, I thought it must *taste* good. So I tried to lick my paws once I was primped and combed.

Bleeeeeech.

Rex and Blix were so busy splashing each other with soapy bubbles that they didn't notice the sour look on my face.

"Okay, puppies," Nanny Fran said. She held up a pair of clippers. "Time to trim your nails."

I buried my head under my paws. That was my way of saying, *GO AWAY!*

But Annie grabbed one of my paws to help Nanny Fran clip away.

"Hold still," Nanny Fran warned me. Nail by nail, she trimmed and filed. It didn't take as long as I'd thought it would—and it wasn't half as horrible. Afterward, Annie took over. She applied a coat or two of doggy polish. I loved the pink color. It matched my barrette.

When she was done painting my nails, Annie held up a pink bottle and squeezed it in front of my face. Some kind of powder came out.

Acccchhhhhhooooooo!

It tickled my nose. But the powder made my fur smell so nice.

Annie tried to pouf powder onto the other puppies, but they weren't having *any* of that. Rex and Blix both ran away.

"Okay," Annie said with a chuckle. "I guess the boys don't need to smell pretty."

"Jeepers, sis," James said. "Why does everything have to smell good?"

Annie made a face. "Like you'd know!" she cracked. "Your feet are the stinkiest in the whole kingdom."

"Thanks a lot," James grumbled.

"At least you smell yummy, Sunny," Annie said to me. She leaned in and rubbed her cheek against mine. "I'm so proud of you and Rex and Blix. I'm lucky to be your princess. You pups are so thoughtful."

I blushed. *"Rowwf!"* I barked, and nuzzled her right back.

"Hurry up!" James called out. "Mom and Dad said the entire palace is assembling in the great room. We need to get down there."

Quickly, James brushed the top of Rex's coat. Annie helped with grooming Blix. His fur coat needed a little bit more attention. Husky fur got super fluffy after a bath. He looked like a huge black-and-white dust bunny!

BLANG, BLANG, BLANG!

Loud clangs came from downstairs. They sounded so official. They came from the bell the staff rings throughout the castle whenever we are expected to gather downstairs or when there's some kind of emergency.

Our celebration was about to begin!

Annie and James led us down the enormous staircase in the entryway of the palace. The carpet felt soft on our paws. As usual, the banister was polished to a royal sheen.

My goldendoodle fur looked more golden than usual today. I think that was because I was so happy on the inside that I started beaming on the outside, too.

The great room had been polished and set up with the finest candlesticks and little vases of white flowers. Trays of food for the people and puppies were set out on the tables. I saw fruits and cakes and a basket of bread. I smelled meat patties and those little hot dogs in pastry shells.

My stomach could not help itself. It began grumbling from the moment we entered the room. And I was tempted to dive right in! I decided, however, that that wouldn't be very good puppy manners. Not in front of the king and queen.

In one corner of the room sat a few musicians: a harpist, a cellist, and a violinist. They were playing a lovely song. It sounded like birds singing! Rex, Blix, and I plopped down to listen. Well, I listened. Rex and Blix found a snag in the carpet and began playing with that instead.

"Your attention, please!" the butler called out.

"May I introduce the master of the castle: King Jon!"

Everyone applauded politely.

King Jon stepped forward with his wife, the lady of the castle, Queen Katherine.

In the queen's arms was the baby, Rose! Even though I was sitting at a distance from the royal family, I could hear Rose gurgle and coo with my puppy supersense.

This was a ceremony to celebrate Rose and offer our gifts to her, but Annie put the gold mobile, silver rattle, and pink blanket in a package together. It was my job to present it to the queen.

"*Rrrroooowoowooo!*" I barked softly. I was ready to bring the gifts to the baby.

"Your attention, please!" the king announced.

The queen put the baby down into a white bassinet. "We are gathered here this afternoon for a special pronouncement," she announced. " As you know, we are honored to have three fine puppies in our palace."

I felt my heart swell. *I love being loved.*

Rex and Blix stopped playing with the rug. Their ears pricked up, too.

"*Brrrrrufff!*" Rex cried to me. "Get up there, Sunny!" he said, cheering me on.

Annie handed me the package at last. She put the handle of the gift bag in my mouth.

My princess winked at me. "Princess Rose is going to love her gifts. I know it," she said.

"It has come to my attention that you three palace puppies have uncovered a palace secret," the king announced. "Indeed, our secret tower has been opened again after too many years!"

I presented the package to Princess Rose, with Rex and Blix by my side. We were the three musketeers now, after all. As I did, the room exploded in a round of applause. The queen took it and opened it for the baby, of course. Our tails began to wag in perfect rhythm. And then, out of the middle of the happy clapping, came a noise that pierced the air.

"*Waaaaaaaaaaaaaaaaaaa!*"

Everyone quickly covered their ears.

"*Waaaaaaaaaaaaaaaaaaa!*"

Uh-oh. The baby was upset. Without waiting a moment more, we trotted over to the bassinet. Rex, Blix, and I jumped onto a stool and poked our heads in to say hello.

With one quick motion, I leaned down and licked Baby Rose's nose. Rex and Blix leaned over and did the same. Everyone waited to see how Rose would react. Would she cry some more?

"*Geeeeeeeeeeeeeeeeeeeeeeeeee!*" Rose gurgled, and then she laughed. Her face looked round and pink. She was happy again, so we jumped off the stool. But the moment all of us ducked back down, the baby's tears returned.

"*Waaaaaaaaaaaaaaaaaaaa!*"

"*Rrooooowwoo!*" we barked, and jumped back up. *Why are you still crying, Princess Rose?* I thought.

Rex dived across the floor. There was no time to waste! We each took out our special gifts from the package. We could make the baby smile, couldn't we?

First, Rex dropped the rattle into the bassinet. The princess grabbed at it with her stubby little fingers. She shook it!

The princess laughed!

We looked at each other. It was working.

Gently, I held up my gift, the mobile. The princess was mesmerized by the gold puppies twirling at the ends of the mobile. She loved the music that played, too. Queen Katherine smiled warmly.

Finally, Blix, the newest puppy at the palace,

presented the blanket. The queen looked ready
to cry by now, but her tears were of happiness.
Annie and James went over and gave her a hug.

Music played, we barked, the princess squealed.

But, after a few minutes, something unusual happened.

Princess Rose's eyelids fluttered. Her breathing got slower and steadier. Her body relaxed. And Princess Rose fell fast asleep!

The whole room stood there, stunned. She had had trouble sleeping—until now. Annie made the mobile play another tune so Rose wouldn't wake up for a while.

The two nannies stepped in to take care of Rose after that. Along with the queen, Nanny Sarah carried the baby back to the nursery for a longer, peaceful nap.

"Nice job, puppies," Nanny Fran said to us on the way out. "That mobile will look perfect in the nursery. You sure are some thoughtful doggies."

We held our heads up proudly.

After the celebration ended, the king declared that we were each allowed to jump up and grab as many hot dogs and patties at the lunch feast as we wanted. I shoved a few into my mouth at once. Yum! This was palace living!

Rex and Blix stuffed a lot into their mouths, too. Then we nipped some berries off a tray and bit into a few cakes. Annie kept telling me to slow down, that I'd get sick.

But I didn't want to stop.

As I was eating a sweet vanilla biscuit, I spotted something under the table, hiding by the table leg. Sir Michael!

"What are you doing here?" I asked.

He smiled. "Looking for crumbs, of course," he said with a chuckle.

I nudged a chunk of my biscuit his way. All the puppies promised Sir Michael that we'd save him and the rest of the palace mouse family as many crumbs and treats as we could in the future.

Things quieted down much more after lunch was done. Sir Michael took the crumbs back to his family. We settled onto a sofa together: me, Rex, Blix, Annie, and James.

Outside the castle, the rain started up again. We heard the gentle *plink-plink* of drops on the roof and windows.

"Shall we read another story?" Annie asked.

"*Woof! Woof! Woof!*" Rex, Blix, and I barked enthusiastically.

Annie produced our favorite new book: *A History of McDougal Palace.*

Rex barked. He gently poked his snout under the sofa cushion where he'd stored the treasure map earlier in the day.

"What is it?" Prince James asked. "You don't want to read?"

Rex shook his puppy head. *"Woooooooof!"* he barked. *Of course he wanted to read!*

But *before* we did that, we had something important to do for Duff McDougal.

Rex carried the map right over to where Annie sat with the storybook.

"Ah, yes!" she said. "The final riddle from the tower door. Good dog."

Carefully, Annie took the map back and tucked it into the inside cover of the large book. James found a piece of tape to seal it shut and keep it safe.

One day again soon, we'd go on another castle adventure. We'd take out the map and find new treasure. We'd slide down into the belly of the castle and climb up again to the secret tower.

But for now, we'd hang out with our prince and princess and enjoy an afternoon doing what we do best: just being palace puppies.